THIS WALKER BOOK BELONGS TO:

_____

_____

_____

_____

For Catherine

A.B.

For the Coughlans:
Larry, Mary, Enda,
Kevin and Ciara

P.J.L.

First published 1994 by Walker Books Ltd
87 Vauxhall Walk, London SE11 5HJ

This edition published 1996

10 9 8 7 6 5 4 3 2

Text © 1994 Antonia Barber
Illustrations © 1994 P.J. Lynch

This book has been typeset in Poliphilus.

Printed in Hong Kong

British Library Cataloguing in Publication Data
A catalogue record for this book is available
from the British Library.

ISBN 0-7445-4768-7

Catkin

WRITTEN BY
Antonia Barber

ILLUSTRATED BY
P.J. Lynch

WALKER BOOKS
AND SUBSIDIARIES
LONDON · BOSTON · SYDNEY

There was once a cat so small that he could sit in comfort on the palm of a man's hand. He was born to an old mother who lived with a Wise Woman on the top of a round green hill.

"The last is often the best," said the Wise Woman to the old cat, and she named him Catkin because his golden tail was no bigger than the hazel catkins that danced outside her window.

Now at the foot of the round green hill, there lived a good farmer and his wife, who cared for the land around them. And deep inside the hill lived the Little People, who are not born, and who do not die, but are there always.

The farmer and his wife had but one child, a baby girl named Carrie for whom they had waited many long years.

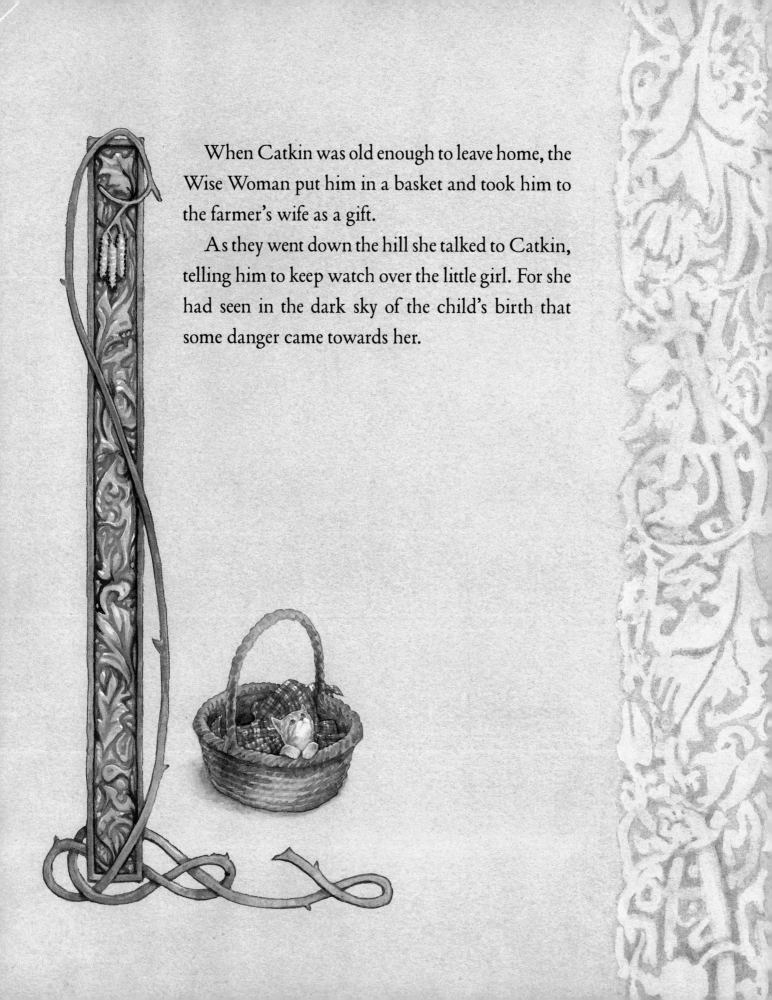

When Catkin was old enough to leave home, the Wise Woman put him in a basket and took him to the farmer's wife as a gift.

As they went down the hill she talked to Catkin, telling him to keep watch over the little girl. For she had seen in the dark sky of the child's birth that some danger came towards her.

Carrie and Catkin loved each other at first sight and where one went, the other was always close by. Through the long summer days they played together, and when night fell the red-gold curls of the child and the golden fur of the little cat lay side by side on one pillow.

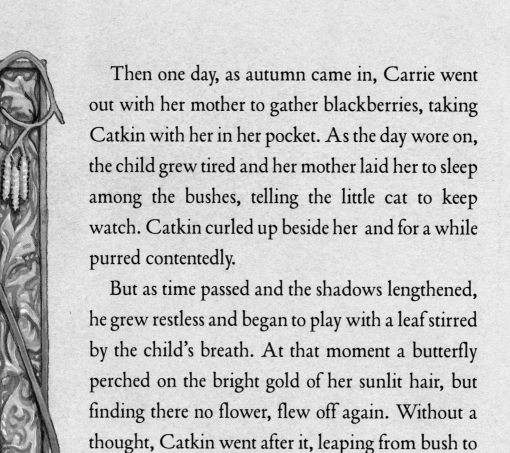

Then one day, as autumn came in, Carrie went out with her mother to gather blackberries, taking Catkin with her in her pocket. As the day wore on, the child grew tired and her mother laid her to sleep among the bushes, telling the little cat to keep watch. Catkin curled up beside her and for a while purred contentedly.

But as time passed and the shadows lengthened, he grew restless and began to play with a leaf stirred by the child's breath. At that moment a butterfly perched on the bright gold of her sunlit hair, but finding there no flower, flew off again. Without a thought, Catkin went after it, leaping from bush to bramble, twisting and tumbling among the fading grasses, seeing only the bright wings caught in shafts of sunlight. Far up the valley he followed and forgot the child.

Then there came a strange quietness upon the air and, pausing breathless, Catkin heard the first faint notes of a faraway music coming from deep inside the hill. His fur rose up in fear and he crouched in the shadows as the soft sound grew.

Out of the green hillside, into the misty sunlight, came the Little People. They were pale and beautiful and laughed together, and some danced to the strange, sighing music. In the midst of them rode their Lord upon a small pony, and beside him his Lady with her hair dark as the night sky and her eyes green as deep water.

Catkin watched in dismay as they moved away down the valley, for he saw that their path would take them to the sleeping child.

He ran after them, but on his tiny legs he could not keep up. They passed on into the mist and out of sight; even the faint sound of their music died upon the air and he was left alone in the silence.

Still he ran on, over rough stones and through sharp thorns, afraid that he would find the child gone. So when he came at last to the place where he had left  her, and saw that she lay sleeping as before, he purred with delight and curled up close beside her. But when he touched her skin it was strangely cold, and as she stirred, she whimpered and pushed him away.

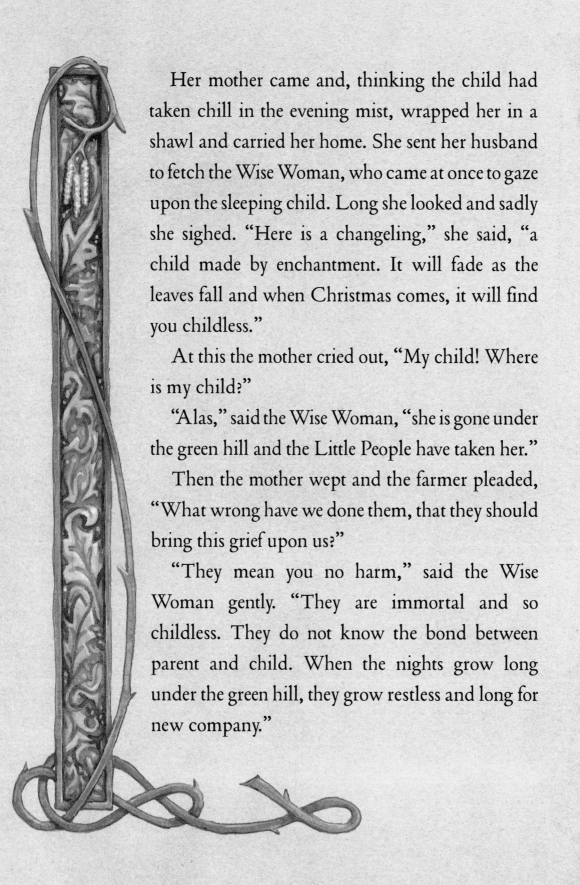

Her mother came and, thinking the child had taken chill in the evening mist, wrapped her in a shawl and carried her home. She sent her husband to fetch the Wise Woman, who came at once to gaze upon the sleeping child. Long she looked and sadly she sighed. "Here is a changeling," she said, "a child made by enchantment. It will fade as the leaves fall and when Christmas comes, it will find you childless."

At this the mother cried out, "My child! Where is my child?"

"Alas," said the Wise Woman, "she is gone under the green hill and the Little People have taken her."

Then the mother wept and the farmer pleaded, "What wrong have we done them, that they should bring this grief upon us?"

"They mean you no harm," said the Wise Woman gently. "They are immortal and so childless. They do not know the bond between parent and child. When the nights grow long under the green hill, they grow restless and long for new company."

"I will go down into the darkness," said the farmer bravely. "I will show them our sadness and beg them to return our child."

But the Wise Woman shook her head, saying, "No man can find the magic door that leads into the green hill." And she sat deep in thought, while the farmer sought in vain to comfort his wife.

Then Catkin, who had hidden himself for shame, crept out from under the Wise Woman's skirts and leapt up onto her knee. He gazed at her with his golden eyes, and looking into the depths of them, she read his thoughts. At last she smiled. "This little one shall go," she said. "By his carelessness was your child taken, and through his courage, she shall come home to you."

"A cat so small!" exclaimed the farmer. "What can he do?"

"It is his size that saves us," said the Wise Woman. "For him the smallest rabbit hole is a highway into the hillside."

"And if he should find her," said the farmer, "how shall a cat plead our cause?"

"In that land of enchantment," said the Wise Woman, "even the beasts may speak and be understood."

She put Catkin upon her shoulder and set out with him up the green hillside. And as they went, she searched her wisdom for what help she could find. "Two streams flow into that hidden land," she told him. "One flows from among the hazel trees and these are the waters of wisdom. The other runs down from the willow pool and these are the waters of forgetfulness. Therefore drink nothing that is offered, but only from the hazel stream." She set Catkin down beside a rabbit hole and parted from him with one last warning: that he tell no one his true name. "For if you speak your name," she told him, "they will weave spells to bind you in that land for ever."

Catkin set out boldly into the black hole and for a long time he wandered in the mazy, earth-smelling darkness. Then he saw a gleam of light ahead and came out into a strange and beautiful world. He found vast caverns within the hollow hill where the walls shone gold and silver and lay reflected in deep lakes of still green waters.

On he went into the very heart of the hill and came, at last, to a splendid palace full of light and glittering with gems.

Here the Lord of the Little People held his revels, with music and dancing and sumptuous foods. And by his side sat his Lady with the child upon her knee.

Watching them from the shadows, Catkin saw that the Lady loved the child, stroking her golden hair and feeding her only the choicest morsels. And he saw also that Carrie loved the dark Lady, putting up her little hands to touch the gentle face. Then he knew that she had drunk the waters of the willow pool and no longer remembered her true home.

When the Little People saw Catkin, they were delighted by the strangeness of a cat so small. The Lady picked him up and laughing set him upon the child's knee. Though Carrie could not remember Catkin, yet she found in him a tiny playmate, and for her sake the little cat was soon in great favour with the dark Lady and her Lord. He found that he could indeed speak to them and be understood, and that life was very good in the land that lies under the green hill.

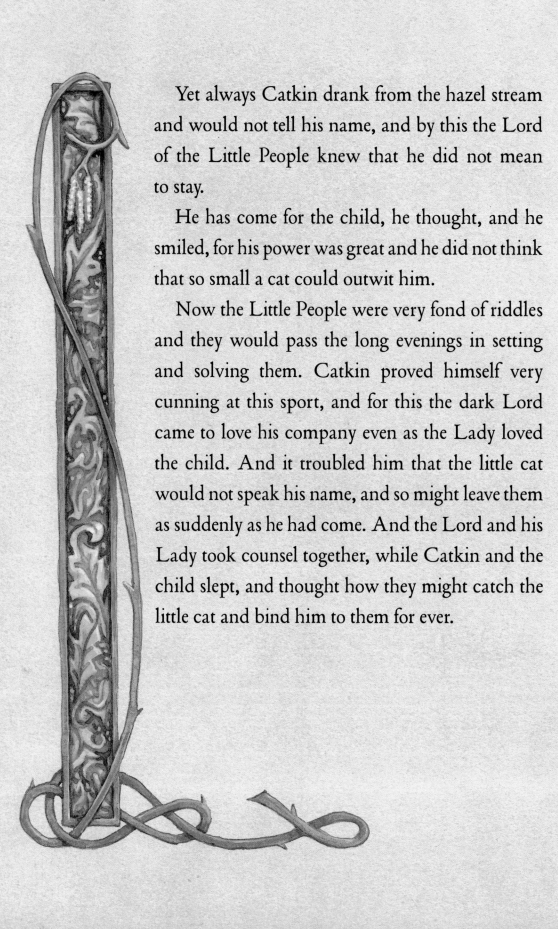

Yet always Catkin drank from the hazel stream and would not tell his name, and by this the Lord of the Little People knew that he did not mean to stay.

He has come for the child, he thought, and he smiled, for his power was great and he did not think that so small a cat could outwit him.

Now the Little People were very fond of riddles and they would pass the long evenings in setting and solving them. Catkin proved himself very cunning at this sport, and for this the dark Lord came to love his company even as the Lady loved the child. And it troubled him that the little cat would not speak his name, and so might leave them as suddenly as he had come. And the Lord and his Lady took counsel together, while Catkin and the child slept, and thought how they might catch the little cat and bind him to them for ever.

On the next day there was a great banquet
to mark the turning of the year, when the days
begin to lengthen and
the nights grow shorter.
After the feasting the
riddles began: there was
much skill in them and
laughter, and Catkin
outwitted them all.

Then the Lord of the
Little People smiled and
his dark eyes were
mocking in his pale face.
He held out his silver cup
to Catkin saying, "Will
you not drink with us now, in friendship?"

And when the little cat would not drink, he said,
"Will you not even tell us your name?"

And when Catkin would not tell it, he said,
"Then it seems to us that you have come for the
child."

Catkin saw that the truth must be told and he
answered, "My Lord, I have indeed come for the

child. It was by my carelessness that you found her unguarded, and her mother weeps for the loss of her."

"Why, so would my Lady weep, if you should take the child from us," replied the Lord of the Little People, "and I should be sad, Little Cat, to lack your company through the long winter evenings. Come, will you not drink with us and forget the past? Have we not made your life pleasant enough that you should seek to leave us?"

"This life is pleasant, indeed," said Catkin sadly, "but there is no peace for me until the wrong is righted."

For a while the dark Lord sat frowning and all were silent. Then he smiled suddenly and it was as if the sun came from behind clouds.

"Then we will give you a challenge, Little Cat," he said. "We shall set you three riddles. If you cannot solve them all, you shall drink from my cup and forget the past. But if you answer all three, then you shall have your way and the child shall go free."

Catkin looked to the Lady, thinking she would cry out. But she sat with her cheek against the child's, smiling, with her eyes cast down. Her smile made Catkin pause and for a moment he was afraid. But seeing no other way, he said, "It shall be as you will, my Lord."

"Why then," said the dark Lord, "hear the first riddle: *So be it, though I am not high, my magic branches sweep the sky.*"

Catkin thought hard and then he said, "My Lord, when you say 'So be it' you tell us what is your WILL: and that which is not high is LOW.

And the tree of enchantment whose branches sweep the sky is the WILLOW."

"Why, so it is!" said the dark Lord laughing, and the Little People marvelled at Catkin's quick thinking. "Now hear the second riddle," said the dark Lord. *"The meadow's wealth I trade for gold, yet wisdom in my fruit I hold."*

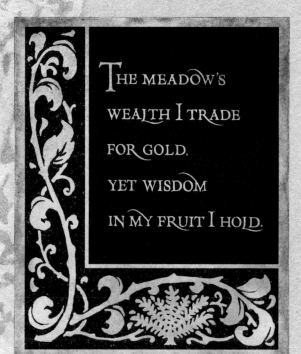

THE MEADOW'S WEALTH I TRADE FOR GOLD, YET WISDOM IN MY FRUIT I HOLD.

Catkin thought harder and for a long time. At last he said, "My Lord, the wealth of the meadow lies in the HAY, and to trade for gold is to SELL. And the tree whose fruit holds wisdom is the HAZEL."

"You are a worthy opponent, Little Cat," said the dark Lord, and his People clapped and cheered at Catkin's skill.

Then the Lady spoke and her eyes were soft upon the child in her arms. "Let the third riddle be mine, my Lord," she said.

"As you will, my Lady," said the dark Lord.

Now though Carrie had forgotten Catkin, yet there was a name she murmured sometimes in her sleep and this the Lady had heard. She looked up at Catkin and her eyes were as deep and as green as the bottomless pools.

"Hear my riddle, Little Cat," she said, and spoke these words: *"Mouse hunter, closer than friend, wind dancer at the bough's end."*

Then hope died in Catkin's heart. For he knew that the mouse hunter is the CAT; and those who are closer than friends are our KIN; and that which dances at the bough's end is the CATKIN. And he knew that to solve the riddle he must speak his name, and if he did so, the child would go free. But once that name was spoken, the dark Lord would have power to hold him under the green hill for ever.

He hesitated and the Lady watched him from under her dark lashes. And she thought, He will not bind himself to save the child.

But Catkin knew that he would have no peace in his heart unless the price was paid. "My Lady," he said, "I speak that which I would rather keep secret. For the answer is CATKIN and the child must go free."

When he spoke these words, the Lady cried out and the child also. Carrie cried out for joy as she remembered her little cat, but the Lady cried for grief that she must lose the child.

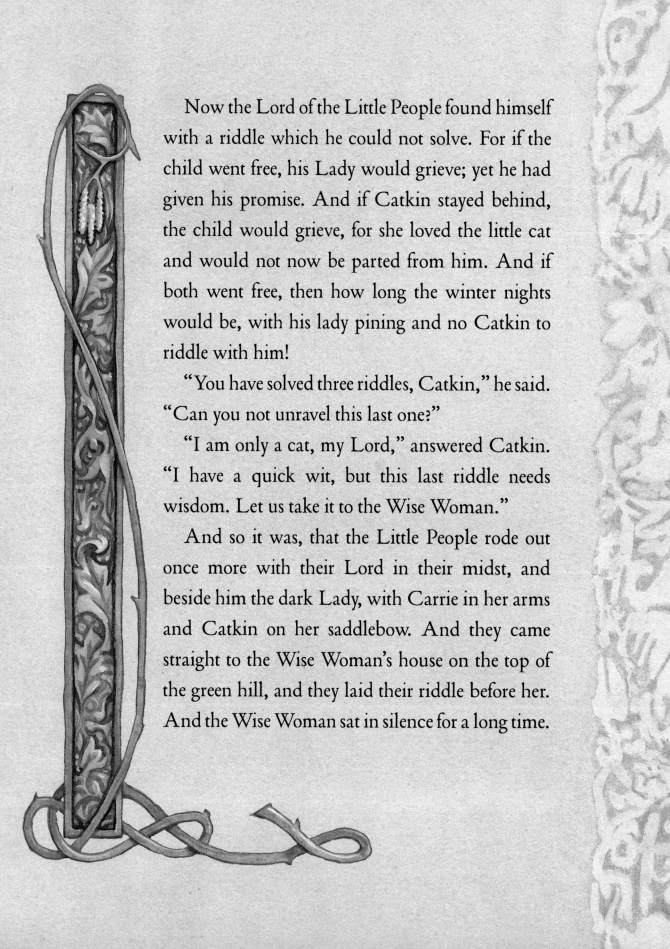

Now the Lord of the Little People found himself with a riddle which he could not solve. For if the child went free, his Lady would grieve; yet he had given his promise. And if Catkin stayed behind, the child would grieve, for she loved the little cat and would not now be parted from him. And if both went free, then how long the winter nights would be, with his lady pining and no Catkin to riddle with him!

"You have solved three riddles, Catkin," he said. "Can you not unravel this last one?"

"I am only a cat, my Lord," answered Catkin. "I have a quick wit, but this last riddle needs wisdom. Let us take it to the Wise Woman."

And so it was, that the Little People rode out once more with their Lord in their midst, and beside him the dark Lady, with Carrie in her arms and Catkin on her saddlebow. And they came straight to the Wise Woman's house on the top of the green hill, and they laid their riddle before her. And the Wise Woman sat in silence for a long time.

Then she said to the Lady, "Though your grief be great, yet greater is her grief that bore the child: therefore Carrie shall return to her mother."

A single tear ran down the Lady's cheek and gleamed in the starlight.

"Yet weep not," said the Wise Woman, "for all is not lost."

Then she turned to the dark Lord and said, "Without the little cat, the child will grieve, therefore Catkin shall go with the child."

And though he had power to bind Catkin to him, the dark Lord bowed his head. "We have sought your judgement, Wise Woman," he said, "and we will abide by it."

"You do nobly, my Lord," said the Wise Woman, "yet all is not lost. Because you have given up your power over them, the child and the little cat shall come to you each year when the nights are longest. Yet you shall not bind them with your magic, and when the first hazel catkins dance in the wind, they shall return from under the green hill to dwell in their own land."

Joy was reborn in the Lady's heart when she heard these words, for though the parting pained her, she knew that she would see the child again. She rode with her Lord away into the starlit night and the Little People returned under the green hill.

Then the Wise Woman set Catkin upon her shoulder and carried the child home. The farmer and his wife saw them coming down the hill, and soon all were gathered into their loving arms.

When they heard of the Wise Woman's judgement, they were generous in their joy, and gave their consent to the sharing. And from that day, all things went well for the good man and his wife. They lived in peace with Carrie and Catkin and the Little People, and the farm on the green hillside flourished.

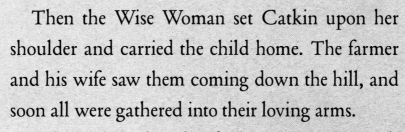

MORE WALKER PAPERBACKS
For You to Enjoy

THE MOUSEHOLE CAT
by Antonia Barber, illustrated by Nicola Bayley

This dramatic and moving Cornish tale of Mowzer, the cat, and Tom, the old fisherman,
who brave the fury of the Great Storm Cat, was the children's choice for the Smarties Book Prize
and winner of the British Book Award (Illustrated Children's Book of the Year).
Shown several times on television, it's now available on video, too.

"A glorious tale... A book to wallow in, read and re-read,
for any age from five or so to very grown-up." *The Sunday Times*

0-7445-2353-2   £4.99

MELISANDE
by E. Nesbit, illustrated by P. J. Lynch

The story of an unfortunate princess by the author of
The Railway Children and *Five Children and It*.

"A joyfully funny fairy tale, illustrated with wit
and traditional richness." *The Guardian*

0-7445-1485-1   £4.99

EAST O' THE SUN AND WEST O' THE MOON
George Webbe Dasent, illustrated by P. J. Lynch

Shortlisted for the Kate Greenaway Medal

A stunning edition of a classic, romantic Norwegian fairy tale –
a kind of Beauty and the Beast with magic and mystery, a curse and a quest,
and trolls with some of the longest noses ever seen!

"A vivid read… Pictures that sear the imagination."
The Independent on Sunday

0-7445-3166-7   £4.99